The Dragon of Krakow

and other Polish Stories

For Malgosia, Anna and Dominick

First published in Great Britain and the USA in 2008 by
Frances Lincoln Children's Books, 4 Torriano Mews,
Torriano Avenue, London NW5 2RZ
www.franceslincoln.com

British Library Cataloguing in Publication Data available on request

ISBN 978-1-84507-752-5

Set in Galliard LT

Printed in Singapore

1 3 5 7 9 8 6 4 2

The Dragon of Krakow

and other Polish Stories

Written by Richard Monte
Illustrated by Paul Hess

FRANCES LINCOLN
CHILDREN'S BOOKS

Contents

Introduction

The stories in this collection prove that there is much more to Poland than the usual picture of a grey land scarred by war and Communism. There are magical tales to be found all over the country – beneath castles and palaces, in towns and cities, in forests and mountains. If you are fortunate enough to travel there and look hard enough, you will find them.

I first started thinking about writing these stories when I was staying in Krakow with my wife nearly ten years ago. We were visiting Wawel Castle, the former home of Poland's kings in the days when Krakow was the capital city. There was a statue of a dragon outside the palace, and I soon realised that sometimes folklore can be more powerful than history. The legend of the Wawel dragon – or Smok Wawelski, as the Poles refer to him – lives on. There is even a dragon's den beneath the castle where tourists flock in their thousands to learn about the creature which once lived under Wawel Hill before Krakow was built. So there it was: a strange tale about a dragon which had threatened to destroy this beautiful city at its birth.

The image stayed in my mind, and later my wife retold the tale to me. Whenever we travelled to Poland – to Warsaw, to the Tatra Mountains, to the Baltic Coast and Gdansk, I was on the lookout for more stories. And I found them everywhere. With the help of my wife's family in Poland, who kindly recalled all those they knew from childhood, a few made their way into this book.

They still strike me as being some of the most unusual folk tales I have ever come across. There are passages as gruesome as anything in the Brothers Grimm, like the king who is eaten by mice as a punishment for his selfish ways. There are humorous episodes, like the two boys who grow as tall as giants and find they can move mountains and pull up enormous forests of oak trees. And there are scenes of great beauty, like the mermaid who lives in an amber palace under the Baltic Sea.

So if you go to Poland, look out for the amber which is sometimes washed up on the Baltic shore. Remember that the reason why Torun gingerbread tastes so good is thanks to the forest bees and their honey – and don't forget that a dragon once lived in Krakow!

Richard Monte

The Dragon of Krakow

A king called Krak decided to build a city at the centre of his kingdom. He travelled widely with his team of advisers looking for a suitable site and eventually settled on a little hill by a river, where trees grew and birds sang.

"What a beautiful place this is!" exclaimed the king. "So peaceful and inspiring. The air is clear, the water is pure – it is the healthiest place I have ever seen!"

A survey was made and Krak's advisers reported back to him. Only one thing troubled them.

"Your Highness, in our opinion the site you have chosen for your city has everything you need for building houses and churches, and the river will bring in trade. We could begin building your castle on top of the hill tomorrow, but something worries us."

"And what is that?" asked the king.

"Under the hill there is a cave, and in this cave

is a huge, green speckled egg. We cannot identify it and we dare not move it, for fear of harming whatever is inside."

"Show me!" said Krak, and they took him into the cave. In one of the damp, warm tunnels the king observed the giant egg.

"Don't worry about it," he said. "Go ahead and build my castle and my city. We will not disturb the egg. Besides, it could well have been here for thousands of years and may never hatch."

So his advisers went away and stopped worrying. They brought in the architects and building began. People moved into the city from all over the kingdom. Shopkeepers set up shops – bakers, wine merchants and shoemakers. Everyone was greedy for trade.

The years passed and Krak named his prospering city Krakow. He was a good king, and the people loved him.

Then one day there was a loud *C-R-A-C-K.*

The king heard the shell of the egg break open. He sent his best men into the tunnels beneath the hill, and half of them returned with the news that a dragon had hatched from the egg. The other half were eaten alive.

"A dragon!" exclaimed Krak. Suddenly the room grew dim and, looking out of his window, he saw

the creature flying, its huge wings almost blotting out the sun.

"Good God above!" exclaimed the king. "That tail alone could wipe out the city with one swish! Its mouth is so big, it could grind this castle into little stones with a single bite!"

"And it's still only a baby, Your Majesty," said an adviser.

"A baby!" the king gasped.

A day came when he looked out of the window of his castle and saw the damage that had been done to his kingdom. The crystal-blue waters of the river Vistula, which wound its snaky path through the countryside below the hill, were no longer crystal blue, but jet-black and full of ash. The clusters of willow trees drooping over the riverbanks were scorched and the sheep with their white winter coats grazing on the hillside were disappearing quickly.

"The nightingale rarely sings in the woods now," lamented the king, "and the air is always smoky."

"Your Highness," said a counsellor, "we fear that the dragon is growing too fast. When it takes a bath in the Vistula, the river floods. The town is under threat."

The king sighed gloomily.

"It seems I am at war, and the sight of my kingdom turned into a battleground unsettles my peaceful heart. What am I to do?"

His advisers told him to start training pages to be knights, and to store weapons in his wine cellar.

"There are no armies at my gates waiting to attack my kingdom," said the king, "yet the jewel in my crown, the beautiful, dazzling, gold and turquoise city of Krakow, with its cobbled streets and wooden churches, with its little green hill and stone castle perched above the river is being attacked" – the king looked out of the window again – "by a dragon!"

At a general meeting, King Krak was informed about the state of his kingdom by a little man reading from a pile of parchment.

"Green fields scorched black.
River full of ash.
Walls of churches burnt and covered in soot.

Sheep eaten and carcasses picked clean.
Economy in ruins.
No trade.
No livestock for farmers to sell.
Market traders staying indoors.
Fishermen complaining that all the fish in the river have died.
Army devastated.
Knights' armour strewn all over the ground.
Swords and shields scattered far and wide.
Dented metal and slaughtered horses everywhere..."

"Anything else?" added the king sarcastically. "The kingdom's in a terrible state. What can I do? Whenever I walk across the wooden floor, I am reminded at every step of the egg which has hatched beneath my feet. Between the gaps in the floorboards, little puffs of steam keep rising and water vapour fills the rooms of the castle. The walls are beginning to crack as the water cools, trickles down them and collects in pools on the floor. Mould and mildew, green and brown, thick, damp and smelly, has begun to form between the bricks. What am I to do?"

"Do not fear, Your Majesty. We have called upon the best knights in Poland and ordered them to fight the monster," came the reply.

That night, the king lay down upon his bed and listened in the darkness. He could hear the dragon most clearly at night-time, stoking its hot, fiery breath, like the devil kindling flames in the dark pits of hell. He could imagine it flicking out its long forked tongue and twisting its great green, scaly body, its tiny eyes as black as death, piercing the red cauldron of its den.

Late at night it would come out, prowling below the hill, plucking sheep from farmyards and cows from barns. It had grown fat on the fruits of his lands and now, like some giant war machine, was breathing fire on the forests and scorching the earth, coughing out dust and ash and cinders like a volcano, leaving it to rise and float back again to smother and choke the little city.

The king tossed and turned, and in his nightmares he saw the city buried in ash and only his little castle peeping out from the ground, a fortress under siege...

He was woken by the sound of little feet pattering up the stairs. The king got out of bed and opened the door. It was one of his smallest advisers.

"More bad news, I'm afraid, Your Majesty.

Two hundred knights dead. An entire flock of sheep consumed. Another orchard burnt."

King Krak sadly shook his head. There was only one thing left to do.

"Go out into the city and tell the citizens that the king offers a reward to any man or woman who can kill the dragon!"

"What will the reward be, Your Highness?" asked the adviser.

"Whatever they wish," said Krak, in despair.

The man went out into the city and, running through the cobbled streets, began announcing the king's reward among the people.

The news reached the ears of Skuba, a poor shoemaker who lived on the outskirts of the city, above a little shop with dirty windows. He had just that moment got up to mend the leaking soles of his boots, but quickly abandoned the task and began to think of a way to outwit the dragon.

He went into a back room of the shop and found an old sheep's hide, a piece of thread and a large needle. Then he went out of the city to a quarry, where there was an abundance of sulphur, and filled several large bags.

Skuba worked through the day, splitting open the sheep's hide, stuffing it full of the yellow sulphur

crystals and stitching it up tightly with the coarse thread. This was harder work than all the pairs of shoes he had made. When it was ready, he brushed up the sheep's white, fluffy coat so that it looked alive. He didn't think the dragon would notice that it didn't bleat any more. That old greedy guts would devour anything which lay in its path. It never stopped to inspect its victims – it just opened those huge cavernous jaws and gulped.

Skuba rubbed his hands. He had finished. Now to tell the king.

The king was standing in his chamber. He had turned his head to the window and was looking up at the clear blue sky and white clouds. At least something was still untouched. The king sighed. But the sky wasn't his kingdom. His kingdom was down on Earth, and it lay in ruins all around him.

"A shoemaker is here to see you, Your Majesty. He says he can get rid of the dragon."

Skuba, carrying the sheep under his arm, explained his plan to the king.

Krak clasped his leathery hands together and asked himself why he hadn't thought of this before. Then, taking the sheep from the shoemaker and inspecting it, he said, "I hope it's lifelike enough." And under his breath he muttered to himself, "The question is, will the beast be fooled?"

Turning back to the shoemaker, he asked, "You packed it with enough sulphur?"

"I stuffed it so full, it almost burst open again, Your Highness," the shoemaker replied.

Once the king was convinced, the hot, spicy little meal was taken down at dusk by several armoured knights and, with four sticks of wood as legs, set up near the entrance to the cave.

***

Night fell. The city slept and the king waited patiently in his castle.

"Nothing's happening! Of all nights, it sleeps on this one – on the very night when I want it to come out and fight!"

"Sssh! I can hear something," said the shoemaker.

Something was indeed stirring in the bowels of the castle. Steam was coming up through the floor. In a moment they both heard the sound of fiery breath and looking out of the window, they could see the night sky lit up red.

They opened the window, stretched their necks out and saw that the sheep had gone. They waited and waited… and those few seconds felt like an eternity.

Suddenly there was a great roar and the long, green, scaly tail swished outwards, clearing everything in its path, as the beast lurched towards the river. There was a loud hiss of water quenching fire, so loud it could have split the heavens, and slowly the water in the Vistula – the filthy, ash-ridden, muddy water – disappeared, and the creature's huge body filled out, until its scaly skin was stretched tight like a balloon.

The shoemaker put his fingers in his ears and the king did the same.

"One, two, three – *BANG!*" they both shouted.

***

The explosion could be heard for miles. The sky was lit up as if a whole bag of fireworks had been let off. People woke, pulled rudely from their dreams, and looked out of their windows in wonder.

The news spread like wildfire. The great dragon was dead! Wise and benevolent Krak, founder of the city of Krakow, had defeated the dragon at last, with the help of a cunning shoemaker.

Peace reigned and the clear-up began. Fresh water filled the river again. The walls of houses and churches were scrubbed and the black soot removed so that the gold and turquoise of the domes and spires shone through once more. Farmers went back to their fields and repaired their fences and broken gates. Merchants started to visit the city again, bringing their wares to the great market in the main square. Wealth flowed back into the kingdom.

The king was happy and carefree once more. He patted Skuba on the back, and said, "I might have wasted my entire kingdom in an endless war with the beast, had it not been for the cleverness of this chap. Now for your reward, young man. What will it be?"

The shoemaker thought for a moment, and then

said: “I’m a poor man who loves making shoes. I live on the outskirts of the city and trade is difficult. All I ask for is the dragon’s skin, so that I can make lots of pairs of shoes for the poor – for I know how it feels to walk on snow and ice in winter with bare feet.”

The king laughed.

“A modest request. I grant it – and you shall have a new shop near the castle, and, I hope, more pairs of shoes to make than there are feet in my kingdom!”

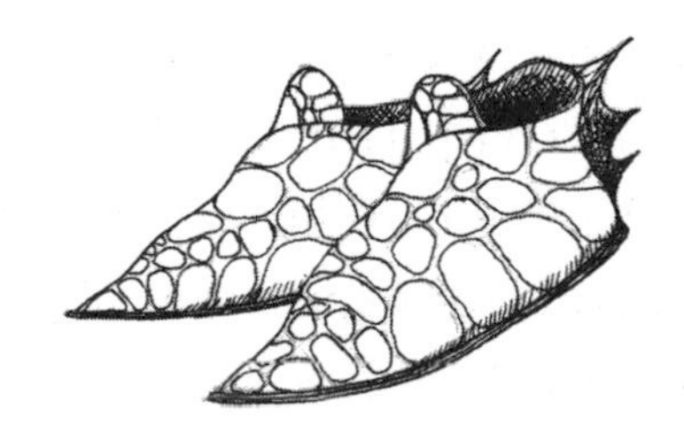

The Amber Queen

Jurata was Queen of the Baltic. Her hair was the colour of amber and her eyes were green and shone like the sea. She was a good queen and all the sea creatures loved her. Her palace, which was made from amber, lit up the sea-bed like a sparkling jewel. Through the windows she kept watch, always ready to go to the aid of those in need.

In return, all the sea creatures helped out in the palace. Sea-horses hung from the curtain rails and wiped the windows. Crabs tidied the cupboards. Cuttlefish polished the chandeliers. Lobsters weeded the garden. Sea cucumbers cleaned the baths and jellyfish hung out the washing. When a fight broke out among the crayfish, the queen was there at once, administering justice with her gentle eyes.

When a sea turtle fell and broke its shell, she let the creature sleep in her bed. When a baby cod caught a cold, she wrapped it in seaweed and nursed the little fish until it was well.

One day, when Jurata was in her coral garden, a shoal of worried plaice swam up to the gate.

"Gentle queen, we need your help. A fisherman has strayed into these waters killing fish for food. Six generations of a halibut family have been wiped out. And the same has happened to a family of cod. The mackerel are fleeing for their lives and one of our friends who escaped from the fisherman's boat told us of a terrible torture in which our cousins have been smoked to death over fires to make food for the fisherman's friends."

The queen of the sea shook her long amber hair.

"How dare a man from land set foot in my waters and capture my fish! You are all under my care and I will not let him harm you."

Jurata went into her palace and began pacing up and down the corridors as she considered what to do. Her eyes glowed like fireballs, her feet stamped like thunder and up on the surface of the sea the fisherman's little boat rocked among the waves as he sailed back to land.

At last she summoned her mermaids.

"I won't let a man kill my fish. He must be punished. We will cast a spell upon him and draw him to us with our singing. Then we will drown him."

She sailed out in an amber boat and the mermaids followed behind her, sitting in enormous yellow shells. They sang a lullaby so enchanting that the clouds stopped and listened and the raindrops danced as they fell.

The fisherman, who had reached land, dropped his nets and turned his head. The sound filled him with a longing for the sea. Then, on the horizon, he saw the amber boat and the entourage of shells, and as they drew closer he saw the queen and smiled, as a feeling of peace filled his heart. Jurata smiled back – and suddenly her anger and desire for revenge melted away.

The queen signalled to her mermaids to stop singing.

"I am Jurata, Queen of the Baltic. I came here to punish you for fishing in my waters – yet now that I see you, I can only forgive you for the things you have done to the creatures of the sea."

The fisherman bowed, then looked up into the queen's green eyes. "And I can only accept your forgiveness and cast away my nets. When I take my boat out to sea, I shall no longer be a fisherman

searching for fish, but a king searching for his queen. I will sail out every evening to see you."

When he finished speaking, Jurata and her mermaids had disappeared. The fisherman stood alone and stared at the sea for an eternity, wondering if what he had seen was a dream.

But it was not a dream, for every evening after that, the queen left her amber palace and she and the fisherman sailed on the water together, under the moon and stars. The queen of the sea sang and the fisherman stroked her golden hair.

But their happiness did not last. One night, the God of Storms saw their little boat floating in the moonlight and was outraged that Jurata had fallen in love with a mortal. He threw a thunderbolt from the sky.

The fisherman's boat was caught in a whirlpool and dragged beneath the waves, and he drowned. The amber palace splintered into a trillion fragments and the queen of the sea was buried beneath it.

Frantically the little sea creatures worked to uncover her. Crabs picked up pieces of amber in their claws and dug away into the night. Lobsters brushed the amber away with their tails. Oysters scooped it up with their shells. But at last, when they found the queen, she was dead.

They dressed her in pink and white coral and buried her in the sand. The crabs dug a hole with their claws and they all wept.

The sea-horses said, "She would not want us to be unhappy. Let us collect the pieces of amber and swim with it throughout the sea."

The oysters agreed. "Let's scatter it far and wide."

"Yes", said the crabs, "and we will make jewels and necklaces in memory of her beauty."

So, even to this day, all the sea creatures remember Jurata by placing pieces of amber on the Baltic shore.

The Gingerbread Bees

There was once a little town called Torun which always smelt of gingerbread. On spring mornings, when the breeze blew towards the river, merchants arriving there could smell the ginger wafting through the streets of bakeries. As soon as they had unloaded their wares, they would rush to have breakfast in one of the little waterfront shops where tea and a gingerbread cake were sold.

The most popular bakery of all was Bartholomew's, run by a man whose name was – not surprisingly – Mr Bartholomew. This old baker had a prosperous business and his reputation for baking excellent cakes was the talk of the whole town.

"Your husband must be a happy man, Mrs Bartholomew. Surely, if anyone has a claim to happiness it would be him," said a customer one day, gingerbread crumbs dropping from her mouth as she spoke.

"Mr Bartholomew – happy?" replied his wife, brushing cake crumbs from her lap. "He won't be happy until the king tells him his gingerbread is the best in the country." She took another mouthful of tea to wash the cake down, then continued, "And he wishes he'd never hired that rascal of an apprentice Bogumil."

It was known that Bartholomew had designs to marry his lovely daughter, with her honey hair and blue eyes, to a wealthy man. It was equally well known that the girl was not interested in the crusty old men who showered her with amber necklaces, silver ribbons and pearl-embroidered gloves in a bid to win her affections, and that her heart was moved more by the bunches of wild flowers and gingerbread hearts given to her by young Bogumil.

"Sack him! That's the only answer, husband. Sack him!" said Mrs Bartholomew one day, as she watched her daughter putting a bunch of freshly-picked flowers into a vase. "For pity's sake, the lad can't even afford to buy his own flowers! What sort of husband would he make our Katarzyna? Sack him, I say!"

Her husband put a hand to his brow. "I can't sack him, my dear. The king is coming to Torun soon and I need all the help I can get. Besides, Bogumil is a good baker."

Light-hearted, happy-go-lucky Bogumil thought of nothing but Katarzyna by day and by night. Although he loved his work at the bakery, there were times when the young man longed only to get away from the hot ovens, and walk dreamily through the forest looking for flowers for his love.

So it was, one morning, that he was walking in a forest outside the town when he spotted a bunch of forget-me-nots growing beside a lake. They were as blue as Katarzyna's eyes. Bogumil was on his hands and knees and about to pick the flowers, when he heard a faint droning sound. He looked up and saw a huge, round, black-and-orange-striped bumblebee drowning in the lake.

Without thinking, Bogumil snatched up a giant sorrel leaf and, leaning out into the water, helped the bee clamber on to it. He put the leaf down upon the bank and, seeing that the bee's wings were wet, moved it into the sun. Soon the bee began to revive and started rubbing its wings. When it was dry, its buzzing grew louder, and eventually it flew off into the forest, leaving the young man alone.

Bogumil was kneeling down again to pick the forget-me-nots when he heard the chirp of a small bird perched upon a twig at the side of the lake. Imagine his surprise when he looked closer, and saw that it was not a bird at all, but a little woman no bigger than his middle finger sitting, not on a twig, but a throne! She wore a tiny crown upon her head.

Bogumil bowed.

The queen spoke, not in a chirp this time, but in a beautiful voice.

"I am the Queen of the Honey-dwellers, and I have come to reward you for your good deed. My people live on the golden honey made by the bees of this forest. When the queen bee fell into the lake, we thought the end had come, for without her the bees cannot work. If she had died, the worker bees would also have died and there would have been no more honey for my people."

Bogumil was speechless.

"Listen to me carefully," she continued, "and you will become the most famous baker in Torun, and your town will be known for ever as the Gingerbread

Town. Remember, when you bake your gingerbread, as well as adding spices, to add a spoonful of honey to the recipe." And she gave him a little pot of forest honey.

Then, before Bogumil could thank her, the queen disappeared. The throne had turned back into a twig and there was a bird perched on it.

Bogumil rubbed his eyes, not sure if he had been dreaming, and, forgetting about the flowers, ran all the way back to town.

The streets were full of people. Bogumil stopped and asked a man what was happening.

"Good God, my boy, where on earth have you been? The king is coming to Torun tomorrow!"

Bogumil went red in the face. The king coming tomorrow! He must get back to the bakery at once.

***

Old Bartholomew was furious when he saw his apprentice. The ovens in the kitchen were already hot and the baker had rolled out his gingerbread dough.

"Where the devil have you been, you young scoundrel? Don't you know the king is coming tomorrow?" he fumed.

His wife shouted, "Every apprentice in town is baking gingerbread, except you. Get to work at once!"

Young Bogumil said sorry a thousand times and quickly gathered together his cooking utensils. He added cloves, cinnamon, black pepper and ginger to his dough, and when the old baker and his wife were not looking, took out the jar of forest honey and added a spoonful to the mixture. He cut the gingerbread into different shapes: knights, flowers, hearts, elks – even bees – and, in remembrance of the little queen, he cut out some tiny crowns too.

Early the next morning, Bartholomew was up rapping on his apprentice's bedroom door.

"Up, you lazy rascal! There's work to be done!"

His wife was already up and about, laying a clean linen cloth over the table outside the bakery. Her husband carried out the trays of gingerbread, eyeing Bogumil's golden creations, which were arranged on a silver tray. That apprentice might have been a rascal, but there was no denying he had a gift for baking. There was such a gleam about his gingerbread biscuits today, they might almost have been made of gold! Bartholomew didn't utter his thoughts out loud. Instead, he shouted, "Bogumil, fetch a ladder my boy, and polish the shop sign until it sparkles."

Bogumil rubbed the old sign until he could see his face in the letters. Then, looking into it, he saw reflected the king's horses approaching the town. There was a great roar from the crowds in the streets and, turning round, he nearly fell off his ladder.

Bartholomew shouted, "Get down off that ladder, boy, and put it away."

"Then clean up your hands and get yourself out here!" added Mrs Bartholomew.

Bogumil meekly did as he was told.

By the time the king arrived at Bartholomew's shop, he and the royal children were already stuffed full of gingerbread. The old baker silently cursed the fact that his shop was in the centre of the town and so far along the royal route. When the king approached, Bartholomew bowed, his wife curtsied and Bogumil held his breath, as the king stepped forward and chose a gingerbread crown from the silver tray. The king's little son and daughter each picked up a gingerbread bee.

The king ate one crown... then another... and another. His children munched their way through a swarm of gingerbread bees and a bunch of gingerbread flowers.

"Who baked these biscuits?" cried the king.

The old baker bowed again, Mrs Bartholomew smiled smugly, and they both pointed proudly at Bogumil.

"This is the most delicious gingerbread I have ever tasted," the king said. He picked up another gingerbread crown. "Tell me, young man, what did you do to make this gingerbread so special?"

Bogumil told the king that he had added forest honey to the recipe, and the king nodded approvingly.

"Ingenious!" he said. Bartholomew smiled. What a clever apprentice!

"Get me a scribe at once," said the king, through a mouthful of Bogumil's biscuits. "I wish to grant this town a royal charter, and bestow upon it the exclusive right to bake honey gingerbread for the King's Market."

Bartholomew patted his young apprentice on the back, forgiving him his errant ways. He promoted Bogumil to senior baker, and gave him his daughter's hand in marriage.

Bogumil was delighted by all this. But he couldn't help wondering if his luck would run out once the little pot of forest honey was finished. He needn't have worried, for one afternoon when he was in the garden of his new cottage, he heard a faint buzzing, and discovered that a swarm of bees had moved into one of his cherry trees. The little queen had sent them so that Bogumil would never have to look for honey again!

His gingerbread got better and better, and when old Bartholomew died, Bogumil took over the bakery and Torun became known as the Gingerbread Town. Bogumil lived happily with his beautiful wife, but he never told anyone about the little Queen of the Honey-dwellers whom he had met long ago in the Forest of Bees.

The Golden Duck of Warsaw

In Warsaw, on cobbled Bednarska Street, there was once a shoemaker's workshop. Above the old shop lived a young apprentice called Janek. He had no family – which was just as well, since he earned so little money from shoemaking. On his days off, Janek often sat looking out of the window, watching the gentlemen in their suits and the ladies in their dresses and dreaming that one day he too would be rich.

He sometimes visited a small inn, where he liked to sit in a corner with his drink and listen to the people around him. It was here, one evening, that he heard something very strange. He strained his ears and caught bits and pieces of the story.

"…A golden duck, I tell you."

"…with gold feathers and a gold crown on its head."

"…It lives in a lake under Ostrogski Palace."

"...Whoever finds this duck will be rich."

"...It is dangerous, very dangerous."

"...To get to the lake, you have to go through endless tunnels."

"...Everyone who has ventured in there has got lost in the winding passages."

Hearing this, Janek rushed home. That night he couldn't sleep, and when he dozed off, he kept dreaming of the golden duck. What if he found it? Just imagine being rich! Surely someone was destined to find that duck, and it could be him!

The next morning at work he kept dropping things, and he even stitched the sole of a shoe on back to front.

"Whatever's got into you today, Janek? Your mind's not on the job!" shouted his master.

As soon as he finished work, Janek returned to his room. He stuffed his pockets with bread and took a little flask of water. Then he sat and waited until dusk.

The street lamps glowed yellow, lighting up Ostrogski Palace. The vault beneath the palace was open. A thin man as tall as a sapling sat guarding the gate. Janek waited for him to take his break, then slipped inside.

Candles lit up the walls. There was a damp, mouldy smell lingering in the air. The steps down were steep at first and covered in slime. Janek tried not to slip. Puddles of stagnant water had collected in the tunnels, and his shoes were soon wet through. As he walked, he nibbled on the bread in his pockets. On and on he went, sometimes wondering if he had taken the right turning. He grew cold and after a few hours the little bread he had left was dry and stale. His flask was empty and he felt thirsty.

"Oh no – I am going to end like all the others before me! Lost! Lost! Lost in the darkness underground!" he cried. His voice echoed back: "*... Lost! Lost! Lost...*"

He buried his face in his hands and had nearly given up hope, when through the gaps in his fingers he thought he saw a white light. He hurried towards it, trying not to slip.

At the end of the passageway he stopped and gasped. Before him was a room divided by polished yellow stone arches. Beneath the arches he saw a bright blue lake that shone like sapphire. And on the water, in the centre of the lake, sat a golden duck.

"So it's true! It's true!" Janek cried.

"It certainly is. I am glad you have found me. Now I will make you rich."

Janek was speechless. A duck that could talk! This was incredible.

"In that bag at your feet are one hundred gold ducats. You may buy whatever you wish with them, but you must spend all the money in a single day."

The young apprentice looked down at his feet. He lifted the bag and felt the weight in his hands.

"Do not share your wealth with anyone. If you do not do as I say, you will go back to being poor."

Janek wanted to thank the duck, but when he looked up, it had vanished. He stared at the lake for a few moments, then looked at the bag in his hand. He undid the string and peered inside. The gold glinted in the light. His heart beat fast as he retied the string.

"I'm rich! I'm rich!" he shouted, jumping up in the air.

But first, he had to find his way out. What use would a bag of gold coins be to him if he couldn't get out again? There were several passages leading away from the lake. Janek chose one and started walking.

Whenever he had to make a choice, he felt it was the right one. Before long he found himself climbing up the steps to the earth above. The door was still open and the guard had gone.

Janek left the grounds of the palace and went back to his room.

***

It was dawn. The start of a new day. Janek had until sunrise tomorrow to spend all his money. If he managed it, the duck would surely give him more money. He divided up the coins into several leather purses and hid them in his biggest overcoat.

Now: off to shop!

His first stop was the market square, where the stallholders were just beginning to put out their wares. Janek spent the entire morning going from stall to stall. He could buy anything he wanted without worrying about the cost. There were Greek olives, Spanish oranges, Italian grapes, French cheese, English mustard, German ham... There were Polish delicacies: sweet rolls with poppy seeds, barrels of honey, prunes in dark chocolate... There were clothes which he had only ever dreamt of wearing: velvet shirts with lace cuffs, silk ties and cravats stitched with gold... He even bought a pair of full-length riding boots from the Turkish merchant, complete with spurs.

At midday he went to the most expensive inn in Warsaw, and ordered the most extravagant food: wild boar, lobster, roast duck stuffed with apples, cranberry sauce, vodka with honey, almond *torte* soaked in rum. As he sat and ate, people whispered among themselves, “Is that some lord over there? He doesn’t seem to care how much he spends.”

They tried to find out who he was and where he had come from, but Janek kept his secret and his money to himself. He swaggered out of the inn bloated and smiling.

Next he bought an expensive diamond from a jeweller on Nowy Swiat. By the late afternoon he owned a horse with silver horseshoes. That evening, he decided to go to the opera and bought the best seat at the Grand Theatre to see Moniuszko's *Halka*. When he emerged from the performance, all the shops were closed. But he still had money in his purse. He wasn't hungry and he didn't need any more clothes.

It was a warm night, so he sat down on a bench in the moonlight.

"How am I going to get rid all this money before dawn?" he said out loud.

"You could give some to me."

Janek looked up. An old beggar had hobbled up to him. He was wearing filthy rags, and he smelt of stale beer and old clothes.

"Have you anything to sell?" Janek asked, remembering his pact with the duck.

"Have I got anything to sell? Now there's a thought!" laughed the beggar. "Well, young man, I've got nothing – except a good heart. I will sell you that."

Janek scoffed. "I don't need a heart. I already have one of my own."

The beggar roared with laughter. "You have a stone for a heart."

Janek felt insulted. "Why do you say that? I have never done anyone any wrong." And he reached into his pocket, pulled out a handful of coins and threw them on the floor at the beggar's feet. "I'll show you my heart! There!"

The earth shook. There was a rumble of thunder and a flash of lightning. The beggar had vanished, and in his place stood a princess with a gold crown on her head, just like the one which the golden duck had worn.

Janek looked down at his clothes. His riding boots had gone. His velvet shirt and silk cravat had disappeared. He was back in his ragged old work clothes again.

"You didn't keep your word, and now you will remain a poor shoemaker's apprentice," said the princess.

Janek blinked, as her words echoed in his ears. Then a wave of relief rushed over him. A great weight had gone from his shoulders.

"What's the point of being rich, if you can't share your riches? I could never be happy like that," he wanted to say – but when he looked up, the princess had vanished.

So Janek went back to his room above the shoemaker's shop and believe it or not, he slept like a log that night – before starting another working day.

Mountain Man and Oak Tree Man

The sound of gun shots echoed through a forest. A bear and a wolf looked at each other and began to run.

"Why does the king always have to go hunting?" gasped the bear, as they hurried off through the trees.

"I don't know. Let's get as far away as possible," cried the wolf.

They didn't stop running until they were on the other side of the forest. It was then that they heard a faint whimpering sound.

"That was no animal cry," howled the wolf.

"You're right. Let's go and have a look," growled the bear.

They hurried towards the crying, until they came to a ring of pine trees. There, beside a tree trunk, lay not one, but two baby boys, and the body of a young woman, who had died giving birth to them.

"Goodness gracious. The poor little mites!" exclaimed the bear, picking them up. "We must get them to safety."

The wolf dug a hole and buried their mother, placing a little cross of twigs in the earth. They gathered up the blueberries she had been picking and ambled home to their cave in the mountains.

"What are we going to do with them?" asked the wolf.

"Well, I'm not handing them over to the king. He'll shoot us on the spot," said the bear. "There's nothing for it. We must bring them up ourselves."

Years passed, and the boys grew older and stronger – so strong, in fact, that one day the bear and the wolf looked at each other aghast.

"Goodness! My boy can pull up trees!" said the bear, looking at a pile of uprooted oaks lying outside the cave.

"That's nothing. Mine has just moved a

mountain!" said the wolf, pointing with her nose to a big gap in the landscape.

"If the king finds out about this, we'll be in for it," said the bear, shaking.

"I think they are old enough to look after themselves!" said the wolf.

When the two boys came back from the forests and the mountains, the bear and the wolf looked at them fondly.

"You have both grown into fine young men. We'll miss you so much," said the bear tearfully.

"Yes, we will. Take care, and don't go pulling up too many oak trees or moving too many mountains, or the king will be after you," added the wolf.

So Mountain Man and Oak Tree Man went out into the world, forgetting everything they had been told. If a dense oak forest blocked their way, Oak Tree Man would pull up the trees by the roots and carve out a path. If a mountain stood in their way, Mountain Man would move it. They went on like this for days and days, until they had moved so many mountains and pulled up so many oak trees that the entire landscape had been altered beyond belief.

***

The king pulled on his beard, looked out of the window of his palace – and fell off his throne. "Karlik, come at once! Someone's stolen my oak forest! How am I going to hunt now?"

The next day he looked out of the window and saw that some of the mountains had been moved. "Karlik, come at once! Someone's stolen my mountains! Are you responsible for this?"

Karlik, the king's adviser, shook his head and squinted through dark, beady eyes. "No master, but I will find out who has done this. He must possess great strength. Perhaps he can kill that terrible dragon."

The king played with his beard. Yes, he had forgotten about their old foe, the dragon. How he would love to be rid of it! The beast had scorched fields with its hot breath, eaten many of the people and threatened to destroy the king's palace.

"Find out who is responsible, and tell him that if he can put his great strength to better use and kill my old enemy, I will give him one of my daughters and my kingdom as a reward."

Karlik scampered off through the corridors of

the palace to find his orange and red magic carpet. He sat down, gave it one quick tug and flew off to find the culprit.

Oak Tree Man was woken by the sound of little feet. At first he thought it was a squirrel, but when he looked closer, he saw that a dwarf in bright red boots had joined them in the glade. He nudged Mountain Man, who blinked in surprise. Karlik had rolled up his orange and red spiral-pattened carpet and was carrying it under his arm.

"Ah! So there are two of you! Good afternoon, gentle giants!" said Karlik politely, peeping up over Mountain Man's shoes. "How would you like to marry the king's two daughters?"

The two giants nodded.

"We'd love to. Just tell us how!"

Karlik put down the carpet and unrolled it.

"Well, if you can defeat the dragon that threatens his kingdom, you will get your reward."

Mountain Man laughed loudly and the ground shook.

"This is a magic carpet. Sit on this and it will take you to the dragon," said Karlik.

At first the two giants thought it impossible that they could both fit on such a small piece of cloth. But as soon as they sat on it, the carpet seemed to grow in size. Karlik clapped his hands and the carpet flew up into the air, carrying the two giants with it. When they looked down, they could see the little man hurrying along below.

"Doesn't it surprise you that I can move so quickly, even though I am so small?" he shouted up at them.

"Yes it does!" Mountain Man shouted back.

"Well, you see my red boots. They are very special. A wizard gave them to me. Once I put them on and start running, each step I take is one mile. If I jump, I can travel two miles."

Karlik demonstrated this and the two brothers had to urge the carpet forward to catch him up.

As the carpet flew over the dwarf again, they shouted down, "Hey there, can we have your boots?"

They were nearing the dragon's lair and landed safely in a clearing. Karlik had taken off his boots and was sitting by a tree.

"How do you know they will fit you?" he asked.

Mountain Man and Oak Tree Man looked worried for a moment. Then, as they tried them on, they both burst out laughing because, like the magic carpet, the boots grew big enough to fit their huge feet.

"The dragon's cave is over there, between those mountains. Good luck – and don't forget to share your boots!" cried Karlik, skipping off back to the palace, well away from any danger.

Mountain Man and Oak Tree Man stared at each other. Then, laughing, each put on a boot.

"I have never worn anything so ridiculous!" said Mountain Man.

"Nor I!" exclaimed Oak Tree Man.

They hobbled clumsily forward.

"I hope these boots work for us!" said Oak Tree Man. It was getting hot and he could smell the dragon's sulphurous breath. He pulled up an oak tree and carried it like a club, in case he needed a weapon.

Then they saw the cave. The ground was littered with old bones and the earth was scorched dry.

"Right. I will climb up on top of the cave and give it a good bang. You hit him with your club when he comes out!" shouted Mountain Man loudly.

The cave shook and a terrible roar came from inside. The dragon was awake!

"Who dares rattle my cave like this!" Out he came, teeth bared and fire circling his tongue.

Oak Tree Man took one look at the dragon and almost dropped his club. It was a good thing he had his magic boot on, because in one jump he had leapt two miles away!

The dragon turned on Mountain Man, who picked up a huge boulder and threw it at the creature. It landed on the dragon's tail. What a roar the beast gave! Mountain Man then used his boot to jump two miles away.

Back in the forest the two brothers discussed what to do.

"That dragon can't move. His tail is pinned to the ground," said Mountain Man.

"Then what are we waiting for! Let's go back and finish him off," said Oak Tree Man, waving his club.

So they used their boots to jump back again.

The dragon was wild with rage.

"You monstrous giants! I'll kill you!" he roared.

Oak Tree Man stepped forward and beat the dragon with his club. Mountain Man threw a huge boulder at him. The dragon let out one last ferocious groan – and expired.

The two brothers strode up to the palace. The king came to meet them and stood on the drawbridge

looking up in amazement at the two giants.

"I saw it all! Come in! Come in! We will have a feast, and you shall marry my daughters! Isn't it a good thing I have two of them!"

Karlik was guest of honour at the marriage ceremony and after dinner, he entertained the guests with wonderful stories of his magic boots.

The next day, at a public meeting, the local farmers and shepherds voiced their worries that the two giants might go on pulling up trees and mountains.

But the brothers reassured them: "Good sirs! Your livelihoods are safe. Never again will we touch the trees or the mountains."

Then they turned to the king. "We have carried out your wishes. We will never move your mountains or your oak trees. But we ask one thing of you."

"And what is that?" asked the king.

"Promise never to hunt the bears and the wolves that live in your forests and mountains."

The king agreed, and when he died, the two brothers banned hunting throughout the land, for they never forgot the kindly bear and the wolf who had brought them up.

Neptune and the Naughty Fish

Among the coral reefs and rock plants of the Baltic Sea, there lived a family called Plaice. They were so plain and dull, the other creatures of the sea never noticed them, but the Plaice family tried to look on the bright side.

"We may not have spots, or stripes, or rainbow-coloured fins like other fish, but at least no one hunts us for food."

Then one day, a clever little Plaice was born. Unlike her brothers and sisters, she was always asking questions about the world.

"What is up there? Does all this water ever come to an end? What are those dark shapes which pass above us across the sea?"

"So many questions for such a little fish!" laughed her granddad, but he didn't have any answers. "Go and see the Salmon. He knows everything."

Granddad Salmon was a wise old fish who lived with his family near a coral reef. He had sailed through many oceans and seen things other fish could only imagine. When the little Plaice started asking him questions, he was surprised.

"Well now, I thought I'd seen everything, but I never thought I'd live to see a Plaice asking questions! Let me tell you about the sea above. Sometimes it can be rough. Ships get caught in violent sea-storms and are cast against the rocks. They sink to the bottom and we call them wrecks. But don't you worry too much, for Neptune the Sea god has forbidden us to go near them."

He knew many sea tales and the little Plaice enjoyed listening to him.

"I would love to swim between the rotting timbers of a sunken ship and hunt for treasure," she said.

The old Salmon nodded, remembering his youth.

"I was like you once, you know. I wanted to find treasure. I was lucky and escaped alive. It's a risky business being a treasure-hunter."

He told the little Plaice how he had seen glass jars

full of wine and olive oil, wooden caskets packed with china, chests of porcelain and sacks of grain, diamond-studded coffers bulging with gold coins, and glittering rainbow-coloured jewels.

"That was in the days before Neptune forbade us to swim among the shipwrecks!"

The old Salmon's stories only made the little Plaice more eager to see the treasures for herself. She spent her days swimming around the old wrecks, crossing waters which were out of bounds, and bringing back questions about the things she had seen.

"What are the big gold circles I saw?" she asked.

"Those are rings," answered the Salmon.

"What are the bigger circles joined together?"

"Bracelets."

"Why do people need rings and bracelets?"

"They think that shiny pieces of metal and stone make them more attractive!" laughed the Salmon.

"I wish I could wear a ring," mused the little Plaice wistfully.

"And where would you stick it? Through your nose? Why can't you just be yourself?" chuckled the Salmon.

***

It was the time of the year when the Salmon left home to visit distant oceans. The little Plaice grew bored.To make her days more interesting, she sought out ships which had sunk to the bottom of the sea. She swam inside them and played with sparkling trinkets. Maybe jewellery would make her more interesting, if only she could find something special.

Other fish warned her, "If Neptune catches you playing in those wrecks, you'll regret it!"

A group of big Cods laughed and jeered, "Haven't you been found out yet?"

The little Plaice waved them away. "I'm not scared of anything! I'm looking for treasure!" she exclaimed.

The big Cods could see that she meant business.

"Well, don't say we didn't warn you!" they shouted back, and quickly swam as far away as possible.

One day, the Plaice decided to go on a journey. The Salmon had once told her of a distant part of the sea where a huge old wreck had lain for thousands of years. It was covered in barnacles and limpets and inside its rusty hull was a jewel-studded chest full of treasure. It was hidden in a room where a chandelier of shells hung from the ceiling.

She swam for days and nights. The sea became deeper and darker and the little Plaice sometimes

stopped to talk to pink crabs and sea-snails with yellow and brown stripy shells.

"You must be new to these waters," said the crabs.

"We haven't seen you before," added the snails.

"I've come to seek out the wreck that lies in this part of the sea."

"Oh, that's over there beyond those rocks. Why do you want to see that rusty old skeleton?" asked the crabs.

"I've been told that a treasure-chest lies inside it. I'm looking for some special jewellery to make myself look more interesting."

"No one has ever dared venture inside. Neptune can see everything, you know!"

"Oh I'm not scared of Neptune," scoffed the Plaice, and with that she swam off towards the algae-covered rocks which the crabs had told her about.

The lights from electric fish lit up the rotting beams of the old wreck. Inside, sea-horses hung from the rafters like lamps. She followed the lights along a corridor. She swam into a room and saw the chandelier of shells hanging from the ceiling, just as the old Salmon had described. In the middle stood a huge chest decorated with carvings of snakes and tongues of fire. It was studded with precious stones: rubies, emeralds, sapphires and diamonds,

which glittered beneath the chandelier.

The little Plaice began knocking against the chest with her snout, mouth and tail, but it would not open, so she swam back through the wreck and went to look for other fish to help her. It wasn't easy. Everyone in the sea was scared of Neptune.

"Why are you all so frightened? Have any of you ever seen him?" she asked.

"Curiosity has already killed the cat! What chance has a nosy little Plaice got?" said the Cuttlefish.

"Seek – and you shall find yourself in deep water!" laughed the Cods.

"Have some sense. You're too young to lose your life," warned the Salmons.

Only a Halibut, a Sole and a blind old Turbot dared enter the wreck.

"Show us where the chest is, and we'll help you

open it, but if Neptune catches you we're not staying around," they said.

The little Plaice was delighted. She wouldn't be so dull and grey once she had those jewels dangling from her body. She led the blind Turbot, the Halibut and the Sole along the dimly-lit corridors of the wreck towards the great room where the treasure-chest lay. The heavy lid creaked as it opened and bubbles of air sailed out into the water and disappeared along the corridors of the abandoned ship.

In her eagerness, she darted inside the chest and started to nose around.

Suddenly the other fish trembled. The entire wreck shook as if an earthquake was shaking the seabed.

"Don't worry. It is only a tremor. It will pass," said the little Plaice.

But the shaking became more and more violent, and they all grew scared.

"This is more than a tremor. Let's go!" shouted the Halibut and the Sole, and dropping the lid, they raced blindly along the corridors, carrying the Turbot between them, in a desperate attempt to find the open sea.

The lid knocked the little Plaice flat. When she looked up, Neptune was sitting beside her. He wore a silver helmet with horns, big black boots and had a bearded face. His eyes were buried under his bushy brows and flashed like lightning. His voice bellowed like thunder.

"So I have caught you trying to steal treasure which does not belong to you!" he roared. "Look at yourself in the lid of that silver chest."

The little Plaice glanced at her reflection. She was now completely flat and her body was covered with reddish-brown spots where the rubies had pressed against her sides.

"Now I will be noticed – even if it isn't quite how I expected to look!" she exclaimed.

"Oh yes you'll be noticed, all right! And one day you will sit nicely on a fisherman's plate, along with your flat friends the Halibut, the Sole and the Turbot," sneered Neptune.

***

When the little Plaice returned to her family, she found that they were also flat with orange spots. "What have you done?" they complained. "Our lives have changed – now everyone is interested in us!"

"Watch out!" shouted her granddad. But it was too late. A fisherman's net swept through the sea and the little Plaice disappeared inside it...

The King who was eaten by Mice

In a castle in the middle of a little wooden town there lived a fat king called Popiel. His belly was so round, it looked like a balloon, and when he stood upright he could barely see his feet! King Popiel loved eating so much that while the people of his kingdom often went without supper, he wined and dined every day. Chickens, ducks, geese, turkeys, rich sauces, freshly-baked bread, cabbages, potatoes, carrots... he guzzled up everything. He often stood in his bedroom looking out of a window at the little wooden houses of the town, watching the people scurrying around like mice, busy working for him. He would put his arm around his wife, whom everyone feared even more than him, stroking her long dark hair, and smile at the thought of his great power.

"Now that my uncles are dead, who can challenge me, Kunegunda, my dear?"

Now, everyone knew that King Popiel had rowed out across the lake one dark night, after a banquet, and, with the queen's help, had thrown some heavy sacks overboard. Furthermore, it was rumoured that these sacks contained the bodies of his uncles, the knights of Gniezno, who had not been seen since they had attended a feast at the castle.

All over the town, people threw up their hands in despair.

"He's murdered his own uncles! What shall we do? It won't be long before he starts murdering us!" cried the miller.

"We've got to do something, or we'll all die of starvation!" shouted the blacksmith.

"I bake bread all day long, and yet I haven't got a crust left to eat," added a baker. "Where does it all go? Up there, to the castle. Just see how round Popiel's belly is. It's full of my freshly-baked baps!"

So the townsmen and women secretly met and wondered what to do. Heads shook as plans to besiege the castle were unveiled.

"The castle's a fortress. We'll be shot before we even reach the walls."

But no one could agree on what to do, until a wrinkled old woman put up her hand.

"I have an idea. We could have a word with

the mice in this town. They could get into the castle."

"Speak to the mice?" Everyone fell about laughing. "Don't be daft, you mad old crab!"

But when a little brown mouse hopped out of her pocket, they all realised the old crab wasn't quite so mad after all. Before anyone had a chance to scream or climb on to a chair, it scurried into the middle of their table and squeaked, "I am so small, I could get into the castle."

The shocked citizens thought for a moment, and then smiled.

"Of course, little mouse, but when you are in the castle, how do you propose to attack the giant Popiel?"

The mouse wiggled its tail and brushed its whiskers.

"I have thousands and thousands of brothers and sisters, all of them armed with sharp claws and pointed teeth, and every one of them is hungry, because that fat giant is eating all their cheese. Now, think about that!"

"It's true," said the baker. "I've seen your brothers and sisters nibbling at the bread in my bakery!"

"And they're in my house, eating the vegetable peelings I throw away!" shouted a washerwoman.

The town councillor waved his hands and called for calm.

"Ladies and gentlemen, think about it! Popiel would never expect to be attacked by an army of mice!"

They whispered for a while, then the councillor looked at the little mouse with the long twitching whiskers and leaning forward, said, "It's a deal. We'll do anything we can to help you train and equip your army, as long as you will fight the king. What do you need?"

The little brown mouse stood up on its hind legs and bowed.

"Enough grain to feed ten thousand of my relatives."

"I suppose I can spare a few sacks," grumbled the miller.

"Enough cheese to feed twenty thousand."

"We might have a few rounds knocking about somewhere," growled a farmer.

"Five thousand of your sharpest needles."

"Five thousand! Good gracious, you don't mean... Oh good gracious me, I'll give you ten thousand..." said the seamstress, unable to contain her laughter at the thought of the king and queen each with five thousand needles in their backsides. "Serve 'em right, I say," she added.

Now everyone could see what the mouse intended, people began thinking how they could help the army.

"I'll make ten thousand mouse-sized coats of armour!" cried the blacksmith.

"I'll pass a law making it illegal to kill any recruit belonging to the Mouse Army," said a councillor, much to the annoyance of the miller's black cat.

"No mousetraps, either!" the mouse squeaked as loudly as it could.

"Absolutely!" cried everyone.

"And no poison!"

"Just as you say, little mouse!"

Then the brown mouse hopped back into the wrinkled old woman's pocket, and the people went back to their work.

***

In the blacksmith's workshop, tiny suits of armour were forged, slowing production of horseshoes for the king's horses. In the miller's yard, five sacks of grain were put aside. In the seamstress's house, thousands of needles were gathered together.

The mice ate their grain, pulled on their suits of armour, took up their needles and headed for the castle. They squeezed unnoticed through a gap in the drawbridge and with their claws made tiny holes in the castle walls for the rest of the army to use. They made their way to the king's pantry and gouged out holes in his rounds of cheese with their sharp little teeth.

The fat king was too busy ordering his servants about to notice anything amiss. Besides, from his windows, it appeared as if everything was normal.

"My soup's too cold. Bring me another pot!" he bellowed.

"My chicken's too hot. Find me a cold chicken!" he roared.

Then one morning, the king jumped up in a terrible rage.

"My cheese has holes in it!"

All the kitchen servants rushed up to the royal chamber to examine the cheese. There was no doubt about it. King Popiel's finest Cheddar, brought by a merchant all the way from England, was riddled with holes.

"There can only be one explanation," yelled the king. "There must be mice in the castle! Get rid of them at once!"

The queen jumped up on a chair at the very mention of the word 'mice', looked out of the window – and immediately fainted. The king caught her in his arms and shouted to his servants for assistance, but they were all gathered at the castle windows, staring out at the most extraordinary sight.

In front of the castle gates stood an army of mice, all dressed in suits of armour and carrying needles in their paws. There were thousands and thousands of them, and they opened their mouths gnashing their sharp little teeth and squealing so loudly that the king was forced to drop his wife, in order to put his fingers in his ears!

When the king surveyed the scene beyond the castle walls and realised what sort of enemy he faced, he laughed.

"I'm not scared of a ridiculous army of mice. Order my knights to get rid of them," he sneered.

But there were no knights left to defend the castle, for King Popiel had murdered them all, and the army of mice was already making its way into the castle grounds.

The sound of tiny feet could be heard scratching at the castle door. Soon a little nose and whiskers, squeezed under the gap between the door and the floor, and a mouse planted itself at the feet of the queen and squeaked. The queen regained her voice and started screaming.

"Oh Popiel! Help! Help!" she shouted, as more and more mice began appearing under the door and out of the floorboards and walls. There were tails and whiskers everywhere. Little paws scampered across the wooden floor and teeth began gnawing at the chairs and tables.

The king and queen tried to think of a place to hide, but the mice followed them everywhere. They climbed on to chairs and into the bed. They filled cupboards and pantries. They chased them all over the castle. The king's round belly wobbled as he struggled up stairways. The queen tried to keep up, but lost her balance and ripped her long dress up to her waist.

"We could try giving them cheese!" she panted, picking herself up from the floor.

So back down the stairs they went to the cellar, where the cheese was kept. The king opened cupboard after cupboard, pulling out great rounds of his favourite cheeses.

"Here – have my finest Cheddar, my best Gorgonzola, my most expensive Stilton!" he yelled, breaking off pieces and throwing chunks at the mice. But nothing worked. The mice weren't interested in cheese any more. They wanted King Popiel and Queen Kunegunda.

"Quick, Kunegunda, we must flee the castle," the king shouted in desperation, pulling the breathless queen with him. They found horses and galloped towards the lake where they had rowed out and thrown the cloth sacks overboard. Neither of them dared look back – and if they had, what a sight would have greeted them! For the mice had gathered together and were marching in unison. King Popiel rowed across the lake like a madman to a tall wooden tower which stood in the middle of an island.

"We'll be safe in there, Kunegunda, my dear. The mice can't swim across water," he said, panting.

But the little creatures were in hot pursuit – thousands and thousands of them brandishing their needles and baring their little teeth. They weren't scared of the water and, as the king and queen climbed out of the boat and scrambled on to the island, the mice were already swimming across the lake.

When they reached the island, they halted and, before going any further, began gnawing at the king's boat so that he could not use it again.

The king and queen quickly climbed the tower and, when they looked down from the parapet, what a sight they saw!

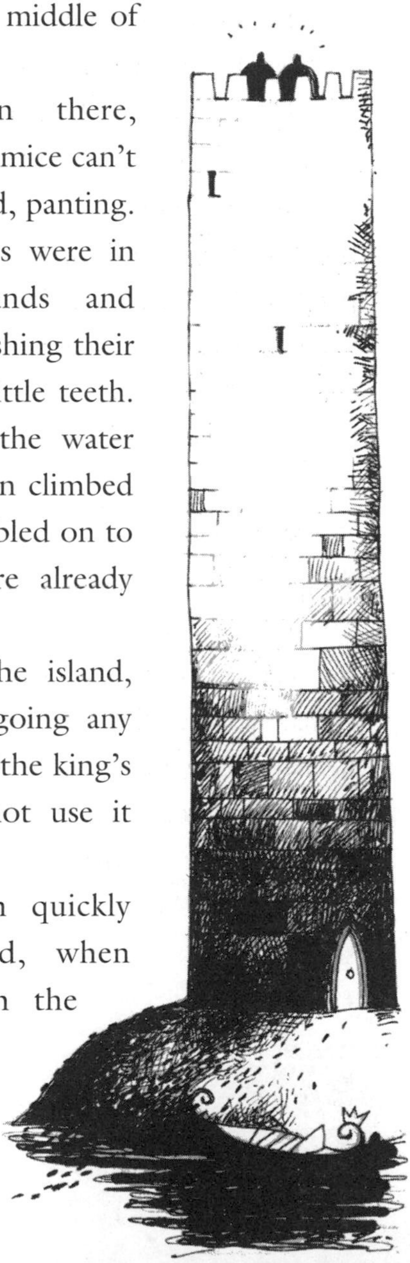

“Oh Popiel, there are mice all over the island! It’s horrible. We’re trapped.”

“I’ll never see any of my cheese again, with or without holes,” lamented the king.

“How can you think of your belly at a time like this?” screamed the queen.

But they didn’t have time to say another word, for the mice were climbing the tower. When the tiny army reached the parapets, the king and queen pulled off their shoes and began frantically trying to beat off the enemy. They leapt up and down waving their shoes in the air. But it was no use. Nothing could stop the mice.

First they began biting the queen’s toes and scratching her gold-painted nails. Then they climbed up her legs and stuck needles in her bottom so that she leapt into the air. They ate the king’s trousers and stuck their needles into his fat rump, until he wished he had never been born. They nibbled at his fingers and at his nose. They nibbled and nibbled until all that was left of the royal pair was their expensive Italian shoes.

***

A loud cheer went up from the people when the army of mice returned. From that day onwards, the mice were allowed to live in peace, away from cats, mousetraps and poison. They were given the tower on the island, which they called 'Mouse Tower', and when the wrinkled old woman died, the little brown mouse who had organised the army swam across the lake and was given a grace and favour home in one of King Popiel's shoes.

About the stories

My wife, Malgorzata Hoscilowicz, has told me many, many Polish stories, including those in this collection. I have also referred to the following:

The Dragon of Krakow
O Kraku, smoku wawelskim i o krolewnie Wandzie, Jozef Ignacy Kraszewski (1812-87).

The Amber Queen
Krolowa Baltyku, Lucjan Siemienski (1807-77). Amber, which is found all over the Baltic sea coast, is the fossilised sap of coniferous trees.

Mountain Man and Oak Tree Man
Waligora i Wyrwidab, Kazimierz Wladyslaw Wojcicki (1807-79).

The Gingerbread Bees
Adapted from the story 'Torunskie Pierniki' by Maria Kruger, *Klechdy Domowe Podania i Legendy Polskie*, edited by Hanna Kostyrko, (published by Nasza Ksiegarnia, Warszawa 1967).
Visit The Gingerbread Museum of Torun at www.muzeumpiernika.pl.

Neptune and the Naughty Fish
Basnie Kaszubskie, from a collection published by M.Arct, 1925.

The Golden Duck of Warsaw
Zlota kaczka, Artur Oppman (1867-1931)

The King who was eaten by Mice
Podanie o Popielu, Cecylia Niewiadomska (1855-1925)

Richard Monte read History at London University. He worked as a newspaper journalist before taking up bookselling and freelance writing. His first novel for children, *The Flood Tales*, was published by Pavilion Books in 2000. He has travelled extensively in Poland, not only to the major cities but also on the Baltic Coast and in the Tatra Mountain region. He has contributed articles on aspects of Poland to the BBC History Magazine and History Today, and has reviewed children's books for the Times Educational Supplement and Carousel. He works as a manager in a branch of Borders Books and lives in St Albans with his Polish wife and two children.

The Prince Who Thought he was a Rooster and other Jewish Stories

Ann Jungman
Illustrated by Sarah Adams
Introduced by Michael Rosen

A Chilli Champion?... a Golem?...
a Prince who thinks he's a Rooster?

Find them all in this collection of traditional Jewish tales – lovingly treasured, retold and carried through countries as far apart as Poland, Tunisia, Czechoslovakia, Morocco, Russia and Germany, with a cast of eccentric princes, flustered tailors, wise rabbis and the oldest champion of all! Seasoned with wit, humour and magic, Ann Jungman's retellings of stories familiar to Jewish readers are sure to delight a new, wider readership.

ISBN: 978-1-84507-794-5

A Fistful of Pearls and other Stories from Iraq

Elizabeth Laird
Illustrated by Shelley Fowles

Having lived in Iraq, award-winning novelist Elizabeth Laird has gathered together a wealth of folk stories spiced with humour, lighthearted trickery and the rose-scented enchantment of the Arabian Nights. Here are nine of the best – stories of boastful tailors, mean-spirited misers, magical quests and a handful of lively animal tales – meticulously researched, elegantly retold and playfully illustrated by Shelley Fowles to reveal the true, traditional heart of Iraq.

ISBN: 978-1-84507-811-9

Hey Crazy Riddle!

Trish Cooke
Illustrated by Hannah Shaw

Why does Agouti have no tail?
How did Dog lose his bone?
Why can't Wasp make honey?

Find the answer to these and other intriguing questions in this collection of vivid and melodic traditional tales from the Caribbean. Sing along to these stories as you discover how Dog sneaks into Bull's party, why Cockerel is so nice to Weather no matter whether she rains or shines, and if the dish really ran away with the spoon!

ISBN 978-1-84507-378-7

The Great Tug of War

Beverley Naidoo
Illustrated by Piet Grobler

Mmutla the hare is a mischievous trickster. When Tswhene the baboon is vowing to throw you off a cliff, you need all the tricks you can think of! When Mmutla tricks Tlou the elephant and Kubu the hippo into having an epic tug-of-war, the whole savanna is soon laughing at their foolishness. However, small animals should not make fun of big animals and King Lion sets out to teach cheeky little Mmutla a lesson...

These tales are the African origins of America's beloved stories of Brer Rabbit. Their warm humour is guaranteed to enchant new readers of all ages.

ISBN 978-1-84507-055-7